Tip and Tucker

Hide and Squeak

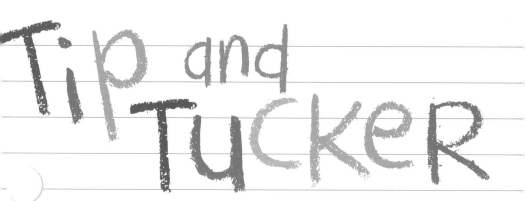

Words by **Ann Ingalls** and **Sue Lowell Gallion**

Pictures by André Ceolin

PUBLISHED BY SLEEPING BEAR PRESS

To my grandmother Phyllys Peterson Lowell,
a caring teacher who loved sharing books
—Sue

Para la familia Lopez, quien significa tanto para mí
(For the Lopez family, who means so much to me)
—Ann

To Gabriel and Grace, for their patience and support.
For Mela, for her invaluable contribution to my career
— André

Text Copyright © 2019 Ann Ingalls and Sue Lowell Gallion
Illustration Copyright © 2019 André Ceolin
Design Copyright © 2019 Sleeping Bear Press

All rights reserved. No part of this book may be reproduced in
any manner without the express written consent of the publisher,
except in the case of brief excerpts in critical reviews and articles.
All inquiries should be addressed to:

Sleeping Bear Press™

2395 South Huron Parkway, Suite 200
Ann Arbor, MI 48104
www.sleepingbearpress.com
© Sleeping Bear Press

Printed and bound in the United States.
10 9 8 7 6 5 4 3 2 1
Library of Congress Cataloging-in-Publication Data
Names: Ingalls, Ann, author. | Gallion, Sue Lowell, author. | Ceolin, André, illustrator.
Title: Hide and squeak / written by Ann Ingalls and Sue Lowell Gallion ; illustrated by André Ceolin.
Description: Ann Arbor, MI : Sleeping Bear Press, [2019] | Series: Tip and Tucker ; book 2 |
Summary: When fearful Tip the hamster falls from the classroom cage
and gets lost in the school, fearless Tucker sets out to find him.
Identifiers: LCCN 2019004066
ISBN 9781534110083 (hardcover)
ISBN 9781534110090 (pbk.)
Subjects: | CYAC: Hamsters–Fiction. | Adventure and adventurers–Fiction. | Schools–Fiction.
Classification: LCC PZ7.I45 Hid 2019 | DDC [E]–dc23
LC record available at https://lccn.loc.gov/2019004066

This book has a reading comprehension level of 1.9 under the ATOS® readability formula.
For information about ATOS please visit www.renlearn.com.
ATOS is a registered trademark of Renaissance Learning, Inc.

Lexile®, Lexile® Framework and the Lexile® logo are trademarks of MetaMetrics, Inc.,
and are registered in the United States and abroad. The trademarks and names of other
companies and products mentioned herein are the property of their respective owners.
Copyright © 2010 MetaMetrics, Inc. All rights reserved.

Honk-shurr, honk-shurr.

BRRIING! BRRIING!

The bell rings.

Tucker wakes up.

He pops out of bed.

The bell scares Tip.
He stays in his igloo.

Kids walk into the room.
They talk and talk.
"What is in the cage?"

"Our new friends," says Mr. Lopez.
"Meet Tip and Tucker."

"Is one hiding?"

"Yes, see Tip's tail? And Tucker snores!"

Who, me?

"Pim, will you read the rules?"

1. Ask the teacher before you open the cage.

2. Bring apples, carrots, or seeds for hamster treats.

3. Fill the water bottle and food dish.

4. Use quiet voices when you are with the hamsters.

5. When you close the cage door, make sure it clicks.

"I like the treats rule," says Tucker.
"I like the quiet rule," says Tip.

"Pim, please put this in the cage."
            CLICK!

"A new place to hide!" says Tip.
"A new chew toy!" says Tucker.

"Time for Music," says Mr. Lopez.

He puts a carrot in the cage.

No click.

"*Hasta luego, chicos,*" says Mr. Lopez.

"See you later, kids."

Tucker takes a bite.

"Do you like school?"

"Too noisy," says Tip.

"I like noise," says Tucker. "And I like naps."

Honk-shurr, honk-shurr.

13

Tip peeks out.
The door swings open.
PLOP!

"HELP, TUCKER!"

Honk-shurr, honk-shurr.
Honk-shurr, honk-shurr.

Tip looks up. Way, way up.
He cannot get back in.

14

CLANG! CLUNK!

"Oh no! I am out of here!"
Off runs Tip.

Tucker wakes up.
The room is quiet.
"Tip?"
No tiny voice.
"Are you hiding, Tip?"

Tucker zips to the igloo.
No Tip there.
No Tip anywhere!
"Where are you, Tip?"

Tip zips down the hall.
Sneakers skip. Flip-flops flap.
He scoots under a door.
No loud noises.
No bright lights.
A good place to hide.

But . . .

No food.

No water.

No Tucker.

Tucker worries.

How will he find Tip?

Tucker leaps out of the cage.

SWOOSH!

He zips around the room. No Tip!

Is Tip in the bathroom? *Sniff, sniff.*
"YIKES! A rat!" yells a girl.
Tucker stops. *Where?*

Tucker zips down the hall.

Big shoes thud.

They stop by Tucker.

Tucker looks up. Way, way up.

It is Mr. Finch. "My, oh my."

A big hand lowers.

Sniff, sniff.

The hand is cozy.

PLOP!

Into the pocket goes Tucker.

But how will I find Tip?

Tip misses his soft bed.

He sees some string.

CHOMP!

A mop falls.

THUMP!

"SQUEAK!"

"SQUEAK!"

Mr. Finch's pocket squeaks back.

The door opens. *CREAK!*

"Tip!"

Tucker peeks from the pocket.

A big hand comes down.
Sniff, sniff.
The hand smells like Tucker.
Tip takes a step.

"Look, Tucker! I am flying!"

PLOP!

Into the pocket goes Tip.
What a good place to hide!

"I am worried," says Pim.
"Me too," says Mr. Lopez.
"Where can they be?"
Mr. Finch peeks in.

"Our hamsters are lost!"

"My, oh my," says Mr. Finch.

"Why is your pocket wet?"

Mr. Finch smiles. "Look who found me!"

"Yay!"

"Mr. Lopez, how did our hamsters
    get out?"
"I put a carrot in the cage,"
    says Mr. Lopez.
"I did not wait for the click.

Lo siento. I am sorry.
I will be more careful next time,"
says Mr. Lopez.

"What a big day!" Tucker says.
"I need a nap."

 Honk-shurr, honk-shurr.

Tip picks up a seed.
"I might like school," he says.

 CRUNCH!

"This is a good home after all."